Thanks,
Mom!

Thanks, Mom!

*A Collection of Stories and
Artwork to Benefit
Habitat for Humanity*

Edited by Gene Stelten
with an introduction
by Millard Fuller

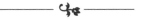

All proceeds received by
Habitat for Humanity from
the sale of this book will be used
to build low-cost housing with
families in need. On behalf of
the hundreds of families on our
waiting lists, thank you in advance
for purchasing this book.

PEACHTREE
ATLANTA

Published by
PEACHTREE PUBLISHERS, LTD.
494 Armour Circle N.E.
Atlanta GA 30324-4088
www.peachtree-online.com

Jacket and book design by Loraine M. Balcsik
Jacket illustration by Gail Tribble
Composition by Robin Sherman

Manufactured in the United States of America

10 9 8 7 6 5 4 3 2 1
First printing

Library of Congress Cataloging-in-Publication Data

Thanks, mom! : a collection of stories and artwork to benefit Habitat for Humanity / edited by Gene Stelten with an introduction by Millard Fuller.
    p. cm.
    ISBN 1-56145-156-8
    1. Mothers Case studies—Miscellanea. 2. Celebrities—Family relationships—Case studies—Miscellanea. I. Stelten, Gene, 1928-
    HQ759 .097 1999
    306.874'3—dc21

                                        98-43828
                                        CIP

To the memory of my wonderful mother, Rose,
With all my love.
Because of your gifts to me,
My life is richer, deeper, sweeter.

And to all the mothers
Who are giving of themselves in their Habitat homes,
To make richer, deeper, and sweeter lives
For all their families.

—G.S.

Gretchen Stelten

$\mathcal{S}$ometimes we take important people for granted—especially those incredible women who welcomed us into the world and continue to touch our lives every day.

This book is a tribute to those who have cared for us, celebrated our triumphs, and soothed us when we were hurt—women who continue to nurture, support, and love us unconditionally.

If you like, use this space to write a special message to your mother. Thank her for the many gifts she has given you and for the precious lessons she has shared with you. Or you can simply say:

Thanks, Mom!

So, thanks, Mom. I remember…

Contents

4—Nurturing

5—Faith

6—Overcoming Adversity

7—A Family Album

INTRODUCTION

*M*others and homes. When we hear the word "mother," we think of "home." How appropriate that we at Habitat for Humanity, who help families build homes, should dedicate a book to mothers.

In the spring of 1997, when work on this book began, we thought you would like to read a collection of stories from celebrities and leaders writing about their mothers. Then as these generous people sent in their stories, we realized it was a lot more than a random collection of stories. There was a theme developing. Helping others. Hard work. Sacrifice. Lessons from our mothers. Gifts from our mothers.

Mothers like to give to their children, and to their families. At a recent meeting of Habitat homeowners, one mother stood up and said, "My family has been blessed. Every time I hear the furnace come on, I think how blessed we are." Sheri and Bill and their three little children had been in desperate circumstances. They knew what it was like to be cold at night. They had worked very hard to help build their own Habitat house and had just recently moved in with Savannah, Jessica, and Madelin. Sheri was so happy that they were able to give their little girls a warm home, so they would be cold no longer!

It *is* a blessing as more and more families move from derelict houses into good and solid ones. It benefits everyone in the process. The challenge is to accelerate making these transformations. Today, Habitat for Humanity puts a family into a new Habitat house every 45 minutes somewhere in the world. More than 70,000 families now live in Habitat homes in all 50 states and in more than 60 other countries. And we can do more.

It is our sincere hope that, as we honor the mothers within this book, we will call attention to mothers everywhere. Mothers who continue to shape the lives of their children with the "gifts" only they can give.

On behalf of the families who will benefit from this publication, thank you for your contribution in purchasing it. May your homes be enriched by the warm and wonderful stories in this book. And, may you be blessed!

Millard Fuller
FOUNDER AND PRESIDENT
HABITAT FOR HUMANITY INTERNATIONAL

I hear my mother when I'm being my best self—soothing someone else.… My mother's best message was that you take care of other people—whether it's the city of New Orleans, the Democratic party, or a little mutt from the pound.

Cokie Roberts

Becoming a mother makes you the mother of all children. From now on each wounded, abandoned, frightened child is yours. You live in the suffering mothers of every race and creed and weep with them. You long to comfort all who are desolate.

Charlotte Gray

For that's what a woman, a mother wants—to teach her children to take an interest in life. She knows it's safer for them to be interested in other people's happiness than to believe in their own.

Marguerite Duras

Helping others

Abe Gurvin

THE LAST ONE

*A*s I look back, I see that my life has always been filled with music, love, friends, family, ambition, cowboy boots, guitars, dogs, cats, and countless other blessings.

My mom let me leave home when I was twelve years old to pursue my call in the field of music. As with a lot of families, ours comes complete with quirks and glitches. But, without question, it's been Momma who has been the steady, calming force that has somehow kept us together. She can't stand it when people are out of line, or if somebody or something is an outcast. Whether it's a stray musician or just somebody down on his luck, Momma has to spread some extra love around. Besides people, her favorites are mutts and unwanted cats. Her hobby since she was a little girl has been to take some under-loved, neglected, unwanted critter and love it to the fullness of life that it was meant to have.

Just like me, a whole lot of other misfits out in the world owe Hilda Stuart more than we could ever pay her for her unconditional love.

It comes straight from God's gift to her, out of a true momma's heart.

When she loses one of her pets Momma always says, "That's it, that's the last one. They're too much trouble and it hurts too bad to lose them." All of us who know her just let her talk and get it out. We know better. She feels that way until the next one comes along. The last star critters to arrive were Florence and Leroy, two jet black cats that somebody abandoned on the sidewalk of the Florence Road Baptist Church in Murfreesboro, Tennessee. Of course she took them home after church, swearing that she would take them to the shelter the next day. That was two years ago.

In my opinion, God gives people certain gifts. Some people are called to be doctors, lawyers, bankers, farmers; others are called to be artists or poets. But God's gift to Hilda Stuart was a heart full of unconditional love. I know. Over the years, I've shown up at her door in every condition. I have always been welcomed with Momma's unconditional love, a glass of tea, and some understanding. If there is a reward in the hereafter for taking care of critters like me, Leroy, Florence, and countless others, a star of jasper will surely be added to Hilda Stuart's already fully jeweled heavenly crown.

In this world of turmoil and confusion she is truly one of the "last ones" of God's most precious angels. I am so blessed to have a friend and a momma like Hilda Stuart. You wouldn't believe how much I love her.

Marty Stuart
MUSICIAN

P.S. Leroy, Florence, and now Buddy the boxer puppy send their best.

$\mathcal{M}$y mother is my heroine. She is loving, strong, smart as a whip, funny, gracious, kind, tough, loyal, and always dependable. She always made me believe I could do anything, and there is no one who takes greater pride in my life than she does.

She has spent her life trying to improve the world of the mentally retarded and she has done just that. Even though she has tackled trying to change the world, I always knew that she would drop it all for me or any of my brothers at any time.

She is everything I admire and everything I'd love to be. God gave me the ultimate gift when he made me my mother's daughter—I love her.

Maria Shriver
JOURNALIST

Lydia J. Hess

$\mathcal{M}$y mother was an angel.

Our family lived six blocks from the rail-road tracks. During the Depression, the freight trains were filled with hoboes wandering from town to town looking for work. Every day they would come by our house asking for food. My kind mother would always share our food with them.

These people were poor and desperate, but we had absolutely no fear of them. We left the doors unlocked. When they knocked and asked for food, there was no concern that they might break in and steal things.

One day, a hobo said, "Lady, don't you have a lot of people stopping by here?"

8

Homer L. Springer, Jr.

My mother said, "Yes, we do."

"Do you know why?" he asked.

She replied, "Not really."

Then he took her out to the street and showed her a mark on our curb. He said, "Lady, this mark on your curb says that you will feed people. That's why you get so many visitors."

After the man left, I turned to my mother and said, "Do you want me to wash that mark off the curb?"

She replied with words that I will remember for the rest of my life. "No, son, leave it there. These are good people. They are just like us, but they're down on their luck. We should help them."

My mother lived the words of a poem that she had my sister, Bette, and me memorize when we were three or four years old:

> *Help the man who is down today;*
> *Give him a lift in his sorrow.*
> *Life has a very strange way;*
> *No one knows what will happen tomorrow.*

Years later, in 1979 during the Iranian Revolution, two of my employees were taken hostage to assure that our company would remain in Iran and keep the Iranian government computer systems operating.

The United States government could not provide any assistance in returning these men.

We formed a rescue team led by Colonel Arthur Simons.

At that time, my mother was dying of cancer. I went to her with great concern to tell her that I would have to go into Iran to help rescue these men, and there was a good chance that I would never see her again.

I explained the situation and she replied, "These are your men. You sent them over there. They did not do anything wrong. Our government can't help you. It is your responsibility to get them out."

She said these words knowing very well that we might never see one another again.

Our team returned from a successful rescue, and when we walked out of the airport in Dallas, my mother had left the hospital and was sitting in a car by the curb to watch the two men as they were reunited with their wives and children.

She died a few weeks later in April, 1979. The last days of her life were very painful, but she was laughing, smiling, and optimistic until her last breath.

Now, my mother *is* an angel. We think about her every day.

Ross Perot

1/4   Blessed Art Thou Among Women (after käsebier) JMeyer

Jim Meyer

*T*his spring, after a long illness that led her away from us gradually over several years, my family and I lost the extraordinary heart and soul that was my mother. Frankly, I have always felt her immortality was assured—not only theologically, but because she lives on in so many of us who knew her as a permanent spring of earthy, earthly, tough, tart, implacable, astonishing wisdom.

An uneducated woman who never felt comfortable with English, who grew up on a remote farm in Italy without electricity or running water, Immaculata Cuomo was the truest sounding board I ever found, whether the issue was the discipline of one of her grandchildren or the direction of grand public policy.

If, in my stumbling Italian, I couldn't explain a decision to Momma, it was probably a bad idea.

And she always cut to the heart of a matter: "How come you're governor, but everybody still has to wait two hours for a driver's license?"

Like my father, Andrea, Momma didn't spend much time imparting abstract lessons of the world, but, through the simple example of her life—her absolute devotion to family and her sharply unsentimental struggle to make

Diane Borowski

a place for us in America—she taught us all perhaps the most important lesson: that what is right is usually also what is necessary, that in helping one another we almost always help ourselves.

Mario M. Cuomo
FORMER GOVERNOR OF NEW YORK

14

Abe Gurvin

$\mathcal{M}$y mother taught me two very important things to help me get through life. The first was manners. She didn't ask for politeness, she demanded it! And when she saw me deviate from what was proper, it displeased her. When I hear the phrase "it displeases me," it still sends shivers up my spine. I answer "yes ma'am" to telephone operators one-third my age.

The other thing she taught me was the art of giving back. My mother loved the phrase, "Where much is given, much is expected." Helping others was not something you could do, it was something you were *obliged* to do.

Both of these ideals have helped me tremendously.

Ed McMahon
ENTERTAINER

15

Abe Gurvin

$\mathcal{M}$y mother's birthday, Christmas, is symbolic of her human warmth, her giving nature, her noble character, and her high Christian values. She and my father instilled those values in all their children from the earliest age, and she lived to make life better not only for her family, but for everyone she knew, particularly those less fortunate than she.

I recall vividly one incident in my childhood that had a lasting impact on me. Every Sunday after dinner, my parents would pack food, clothing, and books in our car and would drive, with their children, to an orphanage just outside our hometown. One Sunday I saw my

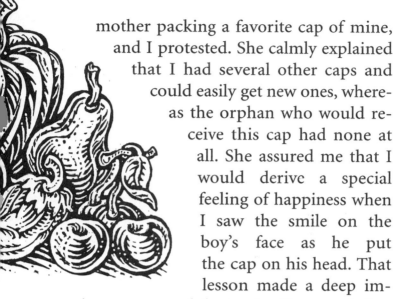

mother packing a favorite cap of mine, and I protested. She calmly explained that I had several other caps and could easily get new ones, whereas the orphan who would receive this cap had none at all. She assured me that I would derive a special feeling of happiness when I saw the smile on the boy's face as he put the cap on his head. That lesson made a deep impression on me, and the truth of her words has certainly stood the test of time as other incidents in my life have validated her words. I consider the wonderful parents that God gave me my greatest blessing, for they both believed it was always more blessed to give than to receive.   17

Michael E. DeBakey, M.D.

Chancellor Emeritus
Olga Keith Wiess
Professor of Surgery
Director, DeBakey Heart Center
Baylor College of Medicine

BIRTH OF THE BLUES

*M*y mother and I disagree about music. Baroque is my favorite. I love the Goldberg Variations. "Too much toodle-te-toodle-te," Mama says. But she indulges me, and when I'm at home we listen to the classical music station. But the minute I'm out the door in the morning, she's up spinning the knob to 106.2, country and western.

When I get home from work in the evening, we sit out on the porch and eat bread and butter and drink tea. She rears back in her reclining chair and sings me the best songs she's heard that day. They are all about the wretchedness of love, the fickleness of women, and the strength of a good man. She has a deep voice and doesn't even try for the high notes. And when she can't remember the words, she just makes up something better. "Now that's good music," she says. I can't disagree.

There's one day she doesn't change the station when I leave the house, though. That's the day they have Listener Request on the classical music station. Every Thursday morning she's on the long-distance phone. My mother has an authoritative manner and an economical telephone delivery.

Mitzi Cartee

"Play me 'The Birth of the Blues' with Benny Goodman and his orchestra," she tells the little man at the radio station.

"I'm sorry, sir," says the man, "but we played that last week."

"Play it again," she says.

"Actually," says the man firmly, "'The Birth of the Blues' is not classical music."

"It is to me," says Mama. "This is 'Listener Request.' I'm a listener. Play it." And he has to do it.

"You know, we've got a Benny Goodman record," I tell her. "Why don't you play the record and leave them alone at the radio station?"

"People need to hear 'The Birth of the Blues,'" she says. "It does them good."

On the first day of summer the classical music station plays a countdown of the top forty listener requests for that year. They start off at 9:00 A.M. with number forty, "The Sounds of Construction and Progress," by Kimio Eto, and work their way down. By afternoon they're in the teens: Mozart's Concerto for Flute and Harp, and Schubert's String Quintet in C Major. At 5:00 P.M. all the faithful listeners are gathered round to hear the big three: Pachelbel's Canon in D, Vivaldi's Four Seasons, and then the number-one hit of this year, and every year since Mama discovered

"Listener Request": "The Birth of the Blues,"
with Benny Goodman and his orchestra. Mama
leans back in her chair and sighs. I don't dare
move or breathe until it's over. "Now that's
good music," she says.

Bailey White

Bailey White
AUTHOR AND NATIONAL PUBLIC RADIO COMMENTATOR

Abe Gurvin

FROM A HABITAT HOMEOWNER

*W*hen I was very young my mother worked for a while as a social worker. One night my twin sister and I overheard our mother on the phone. Her tone was urgent. "Do you have any spare blankets or coats?... Can you give them away?... Can I come pick them up?"

Then mother piled us in the car and we visited family and friends. They all seemed joyful as they brought blankets and coats to our car. Then we drove down a dirt road we had never seen before. We pulled up to a house that was dark.

A little girl answered the door. As the door opened we saw the inside. Only a single candle on the small handmade table illuminated the room. Three little children lived there with their mother. The children at first seemed strangely overweight.

Then I realized they were wearing several layers of clothes.

My mother spoke with their mother. They both had tears in their eyes. I was too young to understand that the reason the house was so cold was because it had no heat. And that was because it had no power!

We were glad when we got back into our warm car. My mother was crying when she said to us, "I hope y'all always have a warm bed to climb into." On that night we visited many other houses on dirt roads, many other children with cold beds.

So years later when I had my own three little girls, and my husband and I found ourselves in desperate circumstances, I remembered the night long ago. I prayed that someone would help us the way my mother had helped others. Those prayers were answered when the sweetest woman visited us from Habitat for Humanity.

I never knew so many wonderful people lived in our community until the hundreds of volunteers came to help us build our own house. My cycle of poverty would be broken by the efforts of these beautiful people. Now every time I hear the heater cut on during a cold night I thank God for Habitat for Humanity, because my little girls are not cold anymore!

Sheri Nunley

2

Mama exhorted her children at every opportunity to "jump at de sun." We might not land on the sun, but at least we would get off the ground.

Zora Neale Hurston

My mother is my root, my foundation. She planted the seed that I base my life on, and that is the belief that the ability to achieve starts in your mind.

Michael Jordan

With a mother of a different caliber, I should probably have turned out badly. But her firmness, her sweetness, her goodness, were potent powers to keep me on the right path.

Thomas Alva Edison

My mother wanted me to be her wings, to fly as she never quite had the courage to do. I love her for that. I love the fact that she wanted to give birth to her own wings.

Erica Jong

Achievement

Leavenworth Jackson

$\mathcal{M}$y mother was an immigrant—only from Saskatchewan, Canada, but still an immigrant. So I was raised on all that "Get Ahead" stuff:

"Make the most of yourself."

"Take advantage of all the opportunities."

"Be a success!"

"Get along with everybody."

"Apple polish, a little bit."

She had been a young teacher in the cold northern prairies of Saskatchewan wheat country—teaching farm children in a one-room school—and she drilled these words into me: "You can be anything you want to be!"

When I was grown, I finally saw where she was raised—small house, outdoor toilet, wood sidewalks. But the family had a piano and my mother learned to play by ear. Her brothers played the fiddle. She could and did recite poetry to us at the dinner table, quoting Shakespeare to teach us moral lessons:

Who steals my purse steals trash...
But he that filches from me my good name
Robs me of that which not enriches him,
And makes me poor indeed.

She improved herself all the time, taking college courses, joining the League of Women Voters and the monthly book club, and serving as president of the PTA. She was encouraging, brave, and always inspiring.

She was also intimidating. When we heard her relate that she was the "Belle of Star City," we took her at her word. The title seemed impressive to me. But then I finally saw Star City, a tiny town of 200 people. Any girl walking by could have been the "Belle of Star City." Whew, what a relief!

But in 1920 Mother got herself to Europe. She was just out of Normal School (that's a school for training teachers) and she was only twenty-one. We saw pictures of her on the deck of the ship in a smart cloche hat. We heard forever about the Tower of London, Madame Tussaud's wax works, the opera *Thais* at the Paris Opera House. One night in Paris she had snuck out to the Folies Bergère with a girlfriend! In her trunk from that European trip with all the snapshots was a short, black, sequined flapper dancing dress with a handkerchief points hemline. We girls all wore that for "dress up" until it was totally wrecked.

She inspired me constantly—and because I was the second little girl and the middle child, I did it all for her.

She'd say: "What you are on the inside shows in your face." I'd run to the mirror every time I did something bad to see if it was emblazoned there.

When I was young and new in Hollywood, she would comment, "You seem to have so much spare time, you could be taking classes at UCLA." I'd say, "Mother, actresses don't have spare time! The phone might ring any minute with an audition!"

She'd say, "I don't know why Katharine Hepburn gets all those parts, you're just as good." I'd scream, "Because, Mother, she's a big star!"

She'd say, "The person you are on the inside is what counts." I'd think, "She's ruined me for life in Hollywood; here it's only what you are on the outside that counts." But "Happy Days" and "Brooklyn Bridge" proved my mother was right!

My mother told such fascinating stories at the dinner table, told everyone's fortunes in the tea leaves. She was very entertaining. I couldn't wait for her to "shut up" so I could get a word in.

My sister and I watched our mother with the ambivalence of all daughters—we balked at her inspiring messages and her darlingness in *29* presenting them. But when she died, we both tried to become her as fast as we could.

Marion Ross
ACTRESS

*A*s a senior in high school, I was a frustrated wide receiver.

"Mom, do you have any idea what it's like to drop a pass right in front of the coach?"

Maybe for a split second you took your eyes off the ball. It happens to the best of them.

"But Mom, I'm second string now, and the quarterbacks won't even throw to me unless there's nobody else open."

Just do your best. Don't give up. You'll get your chance.

Late in the year, I got my chance to make some big plays. Caught a couple of touchdown passes. Even got a partial scholarship to college.

And from there to the pros.

Now my mother is a huge sports fan. She knows all the players, and she's still real big on support and encouragement.

Is there a Hall of Fame for mothers?

Brent Jones
CBS STUDIO ANALYST
SAN FRANCISCO FORTY-NINERS
NATIONAL FOOTBALL LEAGUE PRO BOWL 1993–1996

Abe Gurvin

*A*s they grow to become doctors, lawyers, or even golf professionals, it is not uncommon for appreciative sons and daughters to talk about the sacrifices made by their parents. My mother and father were no different. Perhaps more important than the financial sacrifices my parents made to allow me to fulfill my golfing dreams was the moral support they lent. When my dad and I were out working on my golf game, it didn't matter what time we came home—even if it was ten o'clock at night, Mom would fix us dinner and take care of all the little things mothers seem best at taking care of. My mother was there by my side from the very beginning, so it's

Gretchen Stelten

only fitting that much later in my life, my mother played a great part in my most cherished golf memory.

My mother came to my very first Masters Tournament, but I don't think she went to another Masters until I asked her to go again in 1986. I also asked my sister to go that year, and that was perhaps the only Masters she had attended. I guess I picked a pretty good year to invite everyone, because the first Masters my mother attended in twenty-seven years also became my last Masters victory. Having my family with me that week—my son Jackie caddied for me, my wife Barbara was in the gallery, and my mother and sister were in attendance—did as much to frame the memories of that week as anything. And to have my mother there that week was truly special. She got such a kick out of being interviewed; her face was full of joy and pride. She was as much a part of that week as my birdies on the back nine, my eagle putt at No. 15, or the moment my sixth green jacket was slipped over my shoulders.

My mother turned eighty-nine years young on August 21, 1998, and she's doing fine. She's as sharp as a tack, and she can recall more things than I can. But one thing I will always remember is my mother's joy that week in the spring of 1986.

Jack Nicklaus
PROFESSIONAL GOLFER

Susan Nees

Gretchen Stelten

$\mathcal{M}$y junior year in high school I went to a graduation.

My mother's!

From college. With honors!!

Can you believe it? Well, if you knew my mother, you could. She always told us, "Anything you want to do, you can do."

But can you imagine my shock when my mother told me she would be teaching history at my high school the following year?

"You'll ruin my senior year!" I wailed.

But it didn't turn out that way. As a matter of fact I was extremely proud of her. Proud of her strength and her very deep concern for her family.

Way to go, Mom.

37

J. Veronica Biggins
PARTNER
HEIDRICK & STRUGGLES, INC.

*A*s a very young boy about eight or nine years of age, I was standing with my mother on the verandah of a hostel for black blind women where she worked as a cook. She wasn't very educated, no more than a few years of elementary school. A tall white man in a flowing cassock and a huge black hat swept past us and as he did so doffed his hat to my mother.

It was unheard of in racist South Africa for a white man to raise his hat to a black woman, and a domestic servant at that. The man was Archbishop Trevor Huddleston, CR. I have never forgotten that scene.

The Most Reverend Desmond Tutu
ARCHBISHOP EMERITUS AND CHAIRPERSON,
TRUTH & RECONCILIATION COMMISSION

Abe Gurvin

$\mathcal{M}$y mother has been front and center in my life every step of the way. When I was a young girl, she urged me always to do my best. And while she was there for me to lean on, she also worked to make leaning unnecessary. To this day, she is a strong, wise force in my life, a reckoning star as I have charted my course. She has been my own personal "cabinet," offering constant support and wisdom in life's difficult and challenging moments.

As spiritual leader of the Hanford household, Mother's deep faith in God has been manifested in her many church activities, especially those involving scores of children—her seemingly endless extended family.

Many in North Carolina know her through the helping hand she provided in Dad's

39

business. Others know her as a leader in Salisbury's historic preservation movement, or as a highly conscientious volunteer in many civic organizations. Still others know her for her generosity and dedication to the Cathey-Hanford House, a center for senior citizens, which she donated to the community.

Countless people know Mother for her many quiet, unreported gestures of friendship, her sensitivity and her caring heart, the positive influence and strong encouragement she continually provides. In so many lives, Mother is the constant melody running through our minds, always making us cheerful, always bringing us home.

Elizabeth Dole
PRESIDENT,
AMERICAN RED CROSS

Diane Borowski

STEVE—LOOK!

$\mathcal{M}$y mom has given me some great advice. Two of my favorite sayings are: "No matter what you do, give it your all," and "Be honest with everybody."

My mom likes to cut articles out of magazines and send them to me. They usually have to do with those two pieces of advice.

Just recently she sent me a story about an Olympic champion. When he was in high

41

school, he was on the swimming team. In a very important swim meet, he had just won the race for his school.

His coach thought he had touched the wall. But the swimmer knew he had not touched the wall when he made his turn. So he had a decision to make. He could accept the win or report his error and be disqualified. He decided to 'fess up. He told the truth.

A few years later, he won four gold medals in the Olympics!

My mom had attached a simple note to the article. "Steve—Look." She knows I believe in the advice she has given me. I hope she never stops clipping those articles.

Steve Lundquist
OLYMPIC GOLD MEDALIST,
SWIMMING

42

$\mathcal{M}$y mother was a remarkable lady, and she believed that one should take advantage of every educational opportunity. This meant that even if you weren't feeling too well, you should be in school. The only excuse she would accept for not being in class was death, and she reserved the right to feel the body! Therefore, I maintained perfect attendance in grade school and high school.

Mother also had a kind of farsighted wisdom. When I entered high school, I received the list for available extracurricular activities. I chose tumbling.

When I came home I told Mother about my choice.

"How much tumbling are you going to do in your lifetime?" she said. "Let me see the list."

She looked over the activities on the list, pointed to debating, and handed the list back to me.

43

I became a decent debater and a lousy tumbler.

Donald R. Keough

Donald R. Keough
RETIRED PRESIDENT AND CHIEF OPERATING OFFICER,
THE COCA-COLA COMPANY
CHAIRMAN, ALLEN AND COMPANY INCORPORATED

I'm fifteen years old and I'm in Nagano, Japan, at the 1998 Winter Olympics. Tomorrow I will skate for the gold medal in figure skating. I'm nervous!

My mother reassures me. "You'll do just fine," she tells me. "You've done this program many times. You know every turn, every spin, every jump, as well as you know your own name. And besides, St. Teresa, the Little Flower, will be with you every step of the way."

I feel at ease. I'm calm. And I think about how much my mother has sacrificed to be with me throughout my training, on good days and bad days. Always there for me, to reassure, to strengthen me.

I'm ready to go for the gold!

Tara Lipinski
OLYMPIC GOLD
MEDALIST,
FIGURE SKATING

44

Abe Gurvin

She stood before me, a dolled up pretty yellow woman, seven inches shorter than my six-foot bony frame. Her eyes were soft and her voice was brittle.

"You're determined to leave? Your mind's made up?"

I was seventeen and burning with rebellious passion. I was also her daughter, so whatever independent spirit I had inherited had been increased by living with her for the past four years.

"You're leaving my house?"

I collected myself inside myself and answered, "Yes. Yes, I've found a room."

She gave me a smile, half proud and half pitying.

"Alright, you're a woman. I just want you to remember one thing. From the moment you leave this house, don't let anybody raise you. Every time you get into a relationship you will have to make concessions, compromises, and there's nothing wrong with that. But keep in mind Grandmother Henderson in Arkansas and I have given you every law you need to live by. Follow what's right. You've been raised."

More than forty years have passed since Vivian Baxter liberated me and handed me over to life. During those years I have loved and lost,

I have raised my son, set up a few households and walked away from many. I have taken life as my mother gave it to me on that strange graduation day all those decades ago.

In the intervening time when I have extended myself beyond my reach and come toppling humpty-dumpty-down on my face in full view of a scornful world, I have returned to my mother to be liberated by her one more time. To be reminded by her that although I had to compromise with Life, even Life had no right to beat me to the ground, to batter my teeth into my throat, to make me knuckle down and call it Uncle. My mother raised me, and then freed me.

Maya Angelou
Writer and Scholar

3

Babies don't come with directions on the back or batteries that can be removed. Motherhood is twenty-four hours a day, seven days a week. You can't "leave the office."

Pat Schroeder

There is no such thing as a nonworking mother.

Hester Mundis

If evolution really works, how come mothers only have two hands?

Milton Berle

By no amount of agile exercising of a wistful imagination could my mother have been called lenient. Generous she was; indulgent, never. Kind, yes; permissive, never. In her world, people she accepted paddled their own canoes, pulled their own weight, put their own shoulders to their own plows and pushed like hell.

Maya Angelou

Hard Work & sacrifice

Jim Thorpe

*A*ccording to her height and weight on the insurance charts, she should be a guard on the Lakers.

She has iron-starved blood, one shoulder is lower than the other, and she bites her fingernails.

She is the most beautiful woman I have ever seen. She should be. She's worked on that body and face for more than sixty years. The process for that kind of beauty can't be rushed.

The wrinkles in the face have been earned...one at a time. The stubborn one around the lips that deepened with every "No!" The thin ones on the forehead that mysteriously appeared when the first child was born.

The eyes are protected by glass now, but you can still see the perma-crinkles around them. Young eyes are darting and fleeting. These are mature eyes that reflect a lifetime. Eyes that have glistened with pride, filled with tears of sorrow, snapped in anger, and burned from loss of sleep. They are now direct and penetrating and look at you when you speak.

The bulges are classics. They developed slowly from babies too sleepy to walk who had to be carried home from Grandma's, grocery bags lugged from the car, ashes carried out of the basement while her husband was at war. Now they are fed by a minimum of activity, a full refrigerator and TV bends.

The extra chin is custom-grown and takes years to perfect. Sometimes you can only see it

51

Abe Gurvin

from the side, but it's there. Pampered women don't have an extra chin. They cream them away or pat the muscles until they become firm. But this chin has always been there, supporting a nodding head that has slept in a chair all night...bent over knitting...praying.

The legs are still shapely, but the step is slower. They ran too often for the bus, stood a little too long when she clerked in a department store, got beat up while teaching her daughter how to ride a two-wheeler. They're purple at the back of the knees.

The hands? They're small and veined and have been dunked, dipped, shook, patted, wrung, caught in doors, splintered, dyed, bitten and blistered, but you can't help but be impressed when you see the ring finger that has shrunk from years of wearing the same wedding ring. It takes time—and much more—to diminish a finger.

I looked at Mother long and hard the other day and said, "Mom, I have never seen you so beautiful."

"I work at it," she snapped.

Erma Bombeck
AUTHOR AND HUMORIST

52

❧

Diane Borowski

Betty Jane Trout

$\mathcal{M}$y mother was devoted to her family. She worked very hard to take care of us when we were growing up in Puerto Rico.

My father worked long hours in the sugarcane fields. I can remember him coming home completely exhausted. Mother would sit him down and help him wash his feet, even though she was also very tired from taking care of her children.

Many years later, in the early 1960s, she lived in the Bronx. I was traveling, on the golf tour, trying to make a living.

I had a dream of seeing my mother in a home of her own, in her beloved Puerto Rico. I wanted to repay her, in some small way, for all she had done for me. For all her love for her family.

In 1963, I won the Denver Open. My first tour win. I took the money and built her a new home. And then I moved her to her island home, where she lived the rest of her life.

Thank you, my dear mother. I love you. You taught me that "when you die, what you take with you is what you leave behind."

Chi Chi Rodriguez
PROFESSIONAL GOLFER

I grew up as the youngest of six children right after the Great Depression. My mother never worked outside our home and never learned to drive a car, but she surely worked very hard at running the household. I never heard her complain.

I could tell she wanted more for me and my three sisters because she always stressed the importance of a formal education.

She had many sayings—some that I still use today. This is one of my favorites: "Never sit under a tree that can't give you any shade." Her message was, don't waste your time on things you can't learn from.

Unfortunately, I lost my mother when I was only nineteen years old; she was forty-nine. Perhaps my deepest regret is that she never got to see and enjoy the success I have known. My greatest pleasure would be to treat her to all the beautiful life experiences that she missed by devoting herself so completely to the small world inside her home.

So, each Mother's Day I think of her and the many sacrifices she made so willingly.

Jenny Craig
PRESIDENT / VICE CHAIRMAN, JENNY CRAIG, INC.

Gretchen Stelten

Betty Jane Trout

*M*y mom had only one problem with God's plan.

Ever young of heart, she could see no point in the deteriorating rhythms of advancing age. Her worst fear was that she would be forced to enter a nursing home. It happened. A stroke left Mom paralyzed, and she had to spend her last two and a half years in the place she had dreaded so much.

The first day in the nursing home, she was clearly in a state of anxiety and fear. But the next day, she was serene, smiling, her old self— as beautiful and cheerful as ever. Mom had come to terms with the situation.

I asked her, "You seem at peace. Everything's all right?"

"I can do this for those who suffer far more than I," she answered. Her pain meant something in the wider scheme of things.

She patted my hand. "It's all right, Tommy. It's all right."

She took pain and wove for me a deeper understanding of our connectedness with all humanity. Acceptance of suffering became her gift of redemption.

Father Tom McSweeney
DIRECTOR, THE CHRISTOPHERS

$\mathcal{M}$y mother was born in Springfield, Missouri, in 1923, the second daughter to a gifted carpenter and his hardworking and devoted wife. But as talented as her parents were, they were poor and therefore vulnerable when the Great Depression hit in the 1930s. Life was already extremely hard for them, when my mother's father died suddenly in 1937. She was just fourteen and after the ninth grade, she quit school to help support her mother—and help raise three younger siblings.

My mother grew up doing for others—and working hard. That is what I observed her doing as I grew up—setting an example for me. "Diapers and dishes can wait," she always told me. "Study hard and choose a career," was her constant motto, even though she was a homemaker for most of my growing-up years. My mother sacrificed in more ways than I can count, to see that I got a good education and every opportunity. If I accomplish anything worthwhile it is because of her.

Judy Woodruff
ANCHOR AND SENIOR CORRESPONDENT, CNN

Homer L. Springer, Jr.

Lydia J. Hess

$\mathcal{M}$y mother left Italy in 1925 when she was about sixteen years old to live with her uncles in Vancouver, British Columbia. One of six sisters and one brother whose parents were very poor, she had decided to immigrate to Canada to give some relief to her family. Sadly, she never saw her parents again.

She married my father in 1929, and they began married life only to face the harshness and poverty of the Great Depression. Despite the difficulties my father encountered in obtaining work and earning adequate wages, my mother managed to save a few pennies here and there and those pennies grew into dollars.

When she was in the hospital giving birth to me, she told my father that she had saved some money and that she had hidden it between the mattress and springs of their bed. My dad went home and found $400—a small fortune in his eyes. That amount was enough for them to purchase their first home and it led to a more comfortable life for all our family. My mother's ability to save during such hard times was a remarkable accomplishment, but then she was a remarkable woman.

Frank Iacobucci
JUSTICE, SUPREME COURT OF CANADA

$\mathcal{M}$y mother was eight months pregnant at the time. And there she was, working at the drugstore behind the ice cream counter.

That particular evening, I walked into the drugstore with all the change I had collected from my newspaper route. I needed to have it converted to dollar bills so I could pay my weekly bill on Saturday morning.

I will never forget seeing my mother behind that counter, as tired as she was, working as hard as she was, and carrying a baby. And she was her normal smiling self, upbeat as always.

She was that way with all of us, with my dad and my four siblings, throughout our entire lives, and I feel blessed that she lived to be eighty-three years old.

She was very special in all that she did, not only for her husband and her children, but also for everyone else who came into contact with her.

Bobby Ross
HEAD FOOTBALL COACH, DETROIT LIONS

Carole Boyce

*A*t the 1996 Olympic Trials, when I clinched a berth on the Olympic team, I looked up and saw tears streaming down my parents' faces. I realized then that all of my years of training and all their sacrifices had truly paid off. They saw me reach my goal. I was an Olympian!

When I was younger, my mother drove me back and forth four times a day to practice. She helped me study when I was confused. She kept my spirits up when times were bad.

But most importantly, she loved me unconditionally. I thank God every day for giving me the greatest mom ever.

Amanda Borden

Amanda Borden
OLYMPIC GOLD MEDALIST,
GYMNASTICS

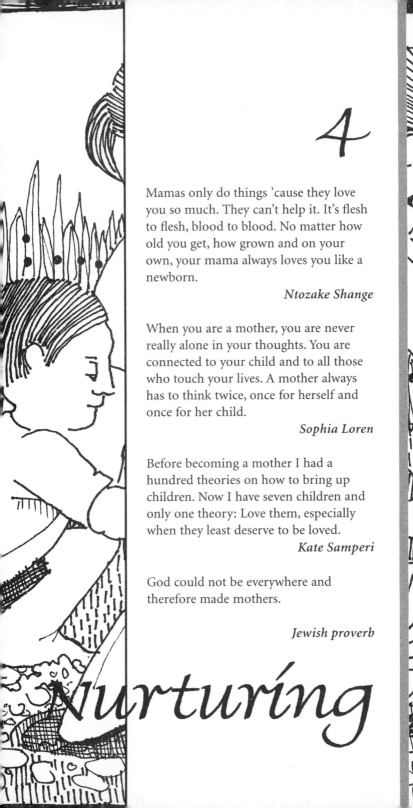

4

Mamas only do things 'cause they love you so much. They can't help it. It's flesh to flesh, blood to blood. No matter how old you get, how grown and on your own, your mama always loves you like a newborn.

Ntozake Shange

When you are a mother, you are never really alone in your thoughts. You are connected to your child and to all those who touch your lives. A mother always has to think twice, once for herself and once for her child.

Sophia Loren

Before becoming a mother I had a hundred theories on how to bring up children. Now I have seven children and only one theory: Love them, especially when they least deserve to be loved.

Kate Samperi

God could not be everywhere and therefore made mothers.

Jewish proverb

Nurturing

Abe Gurvin

When Mother became protective, there was no limit to what she might do. When Walter and I had first left home to go to elementary school, she began going to a Catholic church every day to say novenas for our welfare, despite the fact that she was a staunch Congregationalist. And while I was at Howard in Washington she concocted a way to continue doing my laundry—in New Orleans.

A neighbor on Cleveland Avenue worked on the Southern Railroad, and every week I went

68

to the train station in Washington and presented this man with a bag of my dirty clothes. He took them all the way to New Orleans, a journey of more than a thousand miles. He would deliver them to Mother, then pick up my clean clothes to carry back to Washington when he was ready for his return trip. I thought this was going a little far in motherly protection and dutifulness, but I didn't have the nerve to stop her. Besides, it was better than doing the laundry myself. Fortunately, few of my classmates knew of this arrangement, or I would have been the laughingstock of the dormitory. Those who did know about it were bribed with an occasional piece of homemade angel food cake or oatmeal cookies that were often stashed away with my laundry.

Andrew Young

FORMER AMBASSADOR TO THE UNITED NATIONS

FROM A HABITAT HOMEOWNER

*I*t must have been around mid-July and school was out.

"Mom, I'm bored. Couldn't we go somewhere? Do something?"

"Why don't you read a book? While you're reading, try and imagine that you're there. You can go anywhere. You can do anything." She went to the bookshelf and got down a book on Greek mythology.

Next thing I knew, I was on Mt. Olympus with Zeus and Apollo and a lot of other people I'd never heard of.

A few days later, Ernest Hemingway had me trying to stay afloat with an old man in a small boat, while a huge fish tried to have me for supper.

Well, I was hooked on reading. I must have read twenty more books that summer. Now I read just about anything I can get my hands on.

Because of my mother, I have that special ability to go anywhere, at any time. I'm never bored these days.

Thanks, Mom! I love you.

Chris Schmidt

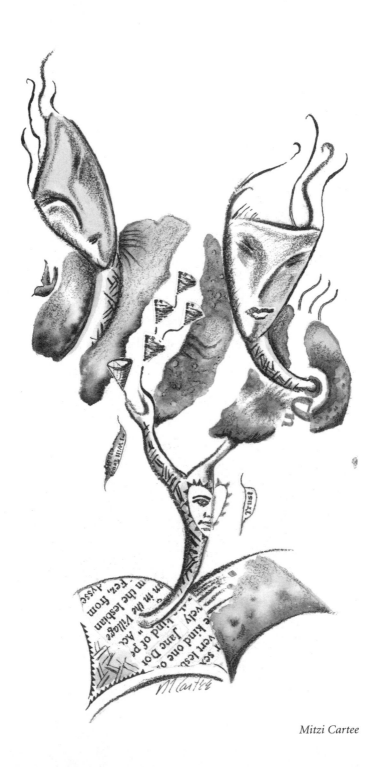

Mitzi Cartee

$\mathcal{M}$ama's minestrone soup was more than just something to eat. It became a symbol of many things. It was security, goodness, health, an economic gauge, a unifier, and an expression of love that was tangible and stuck to your ribs.

There are so many things in life which link me to my past, but few have been more lasting than Mama's soup. For my family, it became an economic indicator more accurate than Wall Street. We could always judge our financial

72

Abe Gurvin

condition by the thickness of the soup. A thick brew indicated that things were going well with the Buscaglias, a watery soup denoted meager, less plentiful times. No matter the abundance of food served in our home, nothing was ever thrown out. Everything ended up in the soup pot.

Mama died about ten years ago, six years before Papa. Somehow, the house was never the same. Someone turned the gas off under the minestrone pot the day after she was buried, and a whole era went out with the flame.

There are so few things that one can really count on these days. We need more minestrone pots in the world. I long for the security, the aroma, the taste. I'm sure there are still such soups simmering in houses all over the world.

Long may they simmer!

Leo Buscaglia
AUTHOR AND LECTURER

*W*hen I was in first grade in North Vancouver, British Columbia, my dad earned $47.00 a week. At the end of each month our family had $12.00 left over for incidentals, like visits to the dentist, doctor bills, or new shoes.

Of course, it seemed to me that we had plenty of money.

So, when I fell madly in love with Harold Fellingham, I asked my mother if I could buy him a real nice Christmas present, like a cowboy hat. She informed me that we didn't have any money. I could not understand that. No money?

Mom said, "I'll bake some homemade cookies, put them in a box, and tie a pretty ribbon on it. It's that or nothing."

I was devastated. When we exchanged names at school, I had literally fought to get Harold's name. And now I was carrying nothing but a box of cookies to school. This could be the end of the romance! When it was time for Harold to open his present, I put my head down on my desk. I tried to hide.

"Wow!" exclaimed Harold, "*Homemade* cookies. My mother never bakes. We buy our cookies at the store." He was thrilled!

My mother—my hero! My mother—the Matchmaker!!

It made me take another look at just how fortunate we were.

Lynn Johnston
CARTOONIST

75

STRAWBERRY JAM

Abe Gurvin

Mother was widowed when I was ten years old. She did a great job of raising three children; she supported us by working in a dry cleaning store and in a defense plant during World War II.

I'm sure life was hard for her, but there were fun times. Like going to pick strawberries on the little farm of our great uncle.

Early every summer, we would all pile into our 1939 Plymouth—the "Grey Ghost"—and head for the farm. My uncle Mike gave each of us a bucket, and we ran out into the field to see who could pick the most strawberries. When we had picked all the ripe ones, we returned to the house for the cooking ritual. At just the right time, my mother added the sugar and a cinnamon stick. The wonderful aroma filled the house!

Then we filled the jelly jars, added the paraffin seal, and we had strawberry preserves for a year. Do you know how wonderful it is to have jelly bread as a snack any time of the day? Or to walk home from school for lunch and know that a jelly sandwich is waiting for you?

Thanks, Mom, for all your hard work. And for the strawberry jam!

77

Thomas J. Fogarty, M.D.
PROFESSOR OF SURGERY
STANFORD UNIVERSITY MEDICAL CENTER
INVENTOR, SURGICAL INSTRUMENTATION

Ramune

*D*id anyone ever give you a gift for no reason, no special occasion? My mother did just that.

I was about nine years old. We didn't have much money, and my mother was looking for a job. She took me with her one day to go to the dry cleaners. There was a jewelry store right next door, and we went in to drop off my mother's watch for repair.

And there it was! A beautiful little ring, with a pretty rose set in "Black Hills" gold, with an itsy-bitsy diamond on either side of the rose. "Isn't it just so pretty?" I said, trying to be very adult in my speech. "So pretty. So pretty."

"I don't think we can afford it," Mother said gently. And we left the store.

Two weeks later, I answered the phone, and the jeweler said, "Your repair is ready." My mother took me with her, and we casually went to the grocery store first, in no hurry to get to the jewelry store. When we arrived there, my mother placed the ring on my finger, and I let out a squeal! I hugged her. My very first piece of jewelry!

Today, the ring is too small to fit any of my fingers. But as I look at it in the palm of my hand, I am reminded of the beautiful, loving look on my mother's face as she presented it to me. This was a truly big deal, because she really couldn't afford it.

She just wanted to give me a gift, for no special occasion.

Summer Sanders
OLYMPIC GOLD MEDALIST,
SWIMMING

80

Homer L. Springer, Jr.

We sit on my mother's shadowed veranda in the cool blue of an August evening while she sorts tomatoes from the garden, and I chirr and natter at her about giving my telephone number to an acquaintance who wants me to come and speak to her book club. I am very busy, I say, and I've had to curtail such speaking engagements.

She smiles meekly and sweetly and agrees to abide by my wishes in the future, and says that she hadn't realized I was so busy. I think, suddenly, looking at her, that in that moment she is a miracle of grace and beauty, the more so in the face of my irritation. It is another gift, one of the last she can give me, the gift of grace.

I wonder if I can properly receive it from her, and if I can ever, myself, achieve that serene and selfless beauty.

All this, all this, is in the air between us as I look at my mother on her twilit veranda, sort- ing tomatoes, smiling her benediction of grace and beauty at me. My love for her nearly stops my heart.

Anne Rivers Siddons

Anne Rivers Siddons
NOVELIST

I have so many wonderful memories of my mother. Sometimes it's fun just to think about her and her rituals.

The daily inspection every day before we went to school:

"Hair combed? Face clean? No jelly stains on the shirt? Brushed your teeth?"

Then the daily lecture:

"What do I always tell you about being respectful? The nuns and the other teachers are dedicating their lives to teaching you. They deserve your respect. They deserve your attention. When I meet with them I always expect to get a good report. Now be on your way."

I can still hear my mother as she worried out loud about our appearance. And as she insisted on our respect for our teachers.

Thanks, Mom.

Joe Paterno
HEAD FOOTBALL COACH, PENN STATE UNIVERSITY
1995 ROSE BOWL CHAMPIONS

Homer L. Springer, Jr.

Before my mother died in early summer of 1976 she wanted to talk about it. The subject of her own death fascinated her, and the long-unremembered details of her childhood and the lives of the relatives who reared her came back to her mind with undimmed freshness.

"Come, sit down and let's talk," she would say as the twilight deepened around her little house in the northwest Florida town of Alford, where she had lived in her girlhood and to which she had returned in the early 1940s.

I couldn't bear to. I didn't want to believe she would not recover from the pains that had begun to rack her eighty-three-year-old body. I didn't want to know where she had put the deed to her house, the only thing she owned, or the name of the man to whom she had been paying her burial insurance for nearly forty years. The stories of the hard times through which her family had lived were painful to me.

"I'll be there in a minute," I'd lie and tackle with renewed frenzy cleaning out the utility room, where she had been saving brown paper bags since World War II. I scrubbed her oven and cleared out kitchen cupboards and replaced shelf papers. In the daytime I dragged the ladder around the house and washed windows with a mindless, obsessive fury.

She sighed and turned her attention to any neighbor who might be passing the gate.

"Come in," she would say hospitably, "and tell me the news." While two old ladies talked, I cleaned madly, relieved that I didn't have to sit still and listen. Now I grieve that I didn't listen. Now I know there's nobody left to tell me things about my family in general but especially the things about my mother, who was the most important person in all our lives for as long as she lived. When she died, I believe in her sleep, one hot afternoon in June, I was overwhelmed with guilt that I hadn't been with her.

She had called Atlanta to tell me, I think. At least she said "that pain" was back in her chest.

"Get Bessie to take you to the hospital," I said, referring to her neighbor and unfailingly kind friend, Bessie Powell. "I'll be there as fast as I can."

"No, I'll wait for you," she said.

"Muv, I'm six hours away," I said, exasperated. "I'll get there as fast as I can but go on to the hospital."

"I may and I may not," she said obstinately and hung up.

Jim Thorpe

Four of my grandchildren were spending time with me in the country and I had obligations at the *Atlanta Constitution,* where I worked, but I made arrangements as fast as I could, and my son, Jimmy, and I took off for Muv's house. We stopped for gas in Columbus and I called her. No answer. I called her neighbor, Bessie.

"She's asleep," said Bessie. "I was just over there and she seems to be resting."

Three hours later we drove up to her gate to find a police car parked under one of the big oak trees and neighbors standing about on the porch and in the yard. Stupidly, I didn't realize what had happened.

"What's going on?" I asked Buck Barnes, who lived across the street from her.

"Your mother has died," he said. "About an hour ago, they think."

It took me a long time, months, maybe years, to realize she had done what she wanted to do. She had no stomach for going back to the hospital and putting up with tubes and needles and the hideous exposure of tests and examinations. She had loved life but she knew she had death coming to her, and she was ready to claim it. I think she walked into her room and got in her bed and willed herself to die.

She may even have been sure the day before that death was imminent because when I went into the kitchen I found that she had done what she always liked to do when she knew that we were coming—"prepare" with turnip greens and a jelly cake, fresh cooked and waiting for us.

Celestine Sibley

Celestine Sibley
AUTHOR AND JOURNALIST

5

When Mother taught us the Lord's Prayer, she put her heart into it. You tried to say it as she did, and you had to put a little of your own heart into it. I believe that Mother, realizing that she was left alone to raise three girls, knew that she had to have a support beyond herself.

Marian Anderson

The God to whom little boys say their prayers has a face very like their mothers'.

J. M. Barrie

A little boy, who was told by his mother that it was God who made people good, responded, "Yes, I know it is God, but mothers help a lot."

Christian Guardian

Faith

When I was five or six years old, my family and I were attending Thornleigh Baptist Church in Sydney, Australia. That particular church holds special memories for me because it is where I gave my life to Jesus. I remember one Sunday we were singing worship songs in church and I looked up at my mum who was standing beside me. I saw tears streaming down her cheeks. I asked her why she was crying and she said there was nothing wrong—she was just worshiping Jesus. In that moment, I think she taught me a huge lesson about the power of worship, one I don't believe I will ever forget.

Although I didn't really understand it then, I now see why she was crying those tears of joy. I've since experienced worship like that and have responded in the same way. I might be worshiping God in my church or in the middle of a concert when tears fill my eyes or start rolling down my cheeks. My mum taught me to love Jesus, to stand in awe of him and express my praise. Worship is delighting in God, whether it be through music, words…or even tears.

rebecca
st james
Phil. 4:8

Rebecca St. James
CHRISTIAN SINGER, AUTHOR, AND SONGWRITER
1997 DOVE NOMINEE, FEMALE VOCALIST OF THE YEAR

Gretchen Stelten

*W*hen I was eight years old, we lived in Arkansas. Back then, my father often worked seven days a week. My mother had us bathed and scrubbed and in church every Sunday.

One day I told my mother, "I need to talk to you." We talked, and she led me to Jesus. The following Sunday I made a public confirmation of my faith. In one sense, it was not terribly eventful for an eight year old. But it was the most important event in my life.

In church we would hear wonderful stories and see slides from all over the world. I always wanted to take part in mission work and never

really was able to do it for the ten years I was busy practicing law. Finally, I was able to go to another country with about forty other people. We went to a remote area of the country and built a church in four days.

Now, when I think about my mother's influence on my life, I am grateful for many things. But mostly I thank her for introducing her eight-year-old son to the sheer joy of doing for others.

John Grisham
NOVELIST

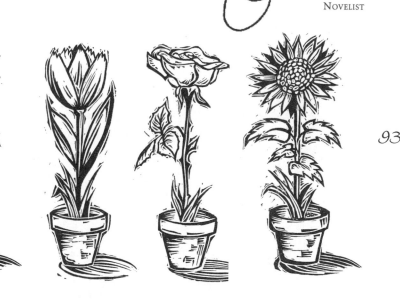

Diane Borowski

Abe Gurvin

Going fishing with my mother is one of my favorite memories of her. She once caught a three-pound bass, which is a rare catch!

My mother learned many ways of the Native Americans regarding fishing and hunting. She was an expert fisherman and hunter.

And I remember learning to pray from my mother. She was very bright and a real good lady.

I look back at her with great admiration and love.

Merle Haggard
GRAMMY AWARD-WINNING SINGER/SONGWRITER

*I*n 1966 I moved from Tallahassee to West Virginia University as an assistant football coach. The first of October rolled around and I realized that I had missed my mother's birthday for the first time ever.

I quickly got on the phone in Morgantown and called my hometown of Birmingham where Mother lived, and asked the florist if they would send her a dozen roses with a message saying Happy Birthday from Bobby. Then I sat down and wrote my mother a letter that went something like this:

Dear Mother,
I want to wish you a Happy Birthday on your sixty-fourth birthday and I miss you up here in West Virginia and I just want you to know that you are the sweetest mother in the world.
                              Love, Bobby
P.S. Mother, I hope you live to be a hundred years old.—BB

I mailed the letter to her and of course the flowers were delivered and I thought nothing more about it. About a week and a half later I got a letter back from my mother.

Dear Bobby,

I want to thank you for the beautiful roses you sent me for my birthday and I also want to thank you for the beautiful note that you sent me. By the way, on your P.S. you mentioned that you hoped that I lived to be a hundred years old. I want you to know that is very nice, but when I was a young girl of thirteen, I accepted Christ as my personal Savior and was guaranteed that I would live forever.

That's my story, and it says it all. Although my mother taught me many things, those were the most significant words she ever gave me.

Bobby Bowden
HEAD FOOTBALL COACH,
FLORIDA STATE UNIVERSITY
1993 NATIONAL CHAMPIONS

Abe Gurvin

OVER THIS YOUR WHITE GRAVE

*O*ver this your white grave
the flowers of life in white—
so many years without you—
how many have passed out of sight?

Over this your white grave
covered for years, there is a stir
in the air, something uplifting
and, like death, beyond comprehension.

Over this your white grave
oh, mother, can such loving cease?
for all his filial adoration
a prayer:
Give her eternal peace—

Pope John Paul II

6

What do girls do who haven't any mothers to help them through their troubles?

Louisa May Alcott

The doctors told me I would never walk, but my mother told me I would, so I believed my mother.

Wilma Rudolph

And for the three magic gifts I needed to escape the poverty of my hometown, I thank my mother, who gave me a sewing machine, a typewriter, and a suitcase.

Alice Walker

It's good for a child to lose as well as win. They must learn in life they are going to be up today and maybe down tomorrow.

Ruby Middleton Forsythe

overcoming
adversity

Diane Borowski

"Your daughter is deaf." The words stunned my family and ruined the holiday. It was Christmas Eve. I was eighteen months old.

Doctors explained that if you can't hear, you can't learn how to talk. You can't get an idea of how you sound. They said I would never go beyond the third grade.

But my mother would not accept that kind of future for me. She chose to believe that a normal life was possible. She decided to concentrate on my potential, not my limitations.

I was blessed to have a teacher for a mother. She spent many hours teaching me as I was growing up. She visited the library to discover how deaf people learn to speak. She would place one of my hands on her throat, to feel the vibration, and the other hand on her lips, to feel her breath.

My mother was very patient. It took me six years to learn how to say my last name correctly!

My mother expected me to achieve my dreams—to use my God-given gifts. She taught me how to sing by showing me how to count at different speeds, depending on the beat of the music. My first song was the Do-Re-Mi song from *The Sound of Music.*

And then I was taught to dance. In ballet class I would again count at different speeds, to match the beat of the music. And then I would move my feet and my arms according to the numbers. One—two—one-two-three.

At the Miss America talent competition, I was able to put it all together in a ballet to a song about Jesus' walk to the cross. I was so happy to honor God, because he has truly blessed me.

And one of my biggest blessings has been my mother, who looks at me as a person with a heart, not a disability.

Heather Whitestone
MISS AMERICA 1995

"It takes little steps to climb a mountain," my mother would say. She had been there all throughout my illness and hospitalization, and now would provide the wisdom that would start me on my road to recovery.

It was during my third season as placekicker for the San Diego Chargers of the National Football League. On my way home from a game I collapsed on the plane.

In the hospital I had two lifesaving surgeries for ulcerative colitis and spent five weeks in intensive care fighting for my life. I was finally released to the care of my parents weighing 123 pounds, down from my 183-pound playing weight. Extremely discouraged, I wondered if I would ever get back to good health.

It was then that my mother offered the "it takes little steps to climb a mountain" advice that I would rely on throughout my recovery. I believe God allowed me to live, recover completely, earn back a spot on the team, make the Pro Bowl, and play seven more seasons.

But it was my mother who offered the encouragement I needed when there didn't seem to be any hope.

Rolf Benirschke
SAN DIEGO CHARGERS HALL OF FAME 1997
NATIONAL FOOTBALL LEAGUE MAN OF THE YEAR 1983

*W*hat impresses me most about my mother is her ability to endure difficult changes and painful losses and still bounce back to face life with an undying sense of optimism.

I remember our family moving, when I was young, from Hummelstown, Pennsylvania, to Fort Riley, Kansas. Mother was going from being a small-town girl surrounded by her friends to being an army wife on a base more than a thousand miles from home. Looking back, I realize how difficult that transition must have been and how much of her life she was leaving behind. Yet what she conveyed to us was not apprehension but anticipation and a belief that the days ahead would be filled with new adventures and new opportunities too vast to imagine.

A few years later my dad was sent to Europe. Mother was left behind with us for a brief time to orchestrate the many details involved in moving an entire family overseas. It was something she had never done before, but she entered into the task with an excitement and enthusiasm that made moving away to a strange, unfamiliar country seem like a great and wonderful adventure.

As an army wife, she would be called on again and again to pack up her family, say good-bye to familiar surroundings, and move on to new, uncharted territory. While there must have been some regret and anxiety on her part, what she imparted to us, her children, was always a sense of excitement, anticipation and promise. Because of her, we learned to see changes as adventures, challenges as opportunities.

Recently my dad died, shortly after their fiftieth wedding anniversary. My mother again was called upon to say good-bye to the familiar and the loved and to move on, this time without the man who had been her companion for half a century. After a period of pain and mourning, she once again came back with the spirit I've come to know so well, strengthened by the same simple truths she'd taught her children. *Every day is a day God has given us. Live each one to the fullest. And always face what lies ahead with faith, hope, and undying optimism.*

It is that spirit—learned from my mother—that helped shape my life.

Newt Gingrich
FORMER SPEAKER
UNITED STATES HOUSE OF REPRESENTATIVES

Speaker Gingrich is an enthusiastic supporter of Habitat for Humanity. He has sponsored two Habitat houses in Georgia, raised money for numerous Habitat chapters throughout the country, and personally helped build nine Habitat homes. As a result of his commitment, Members of Congress recently built two Habitat houses in Washington, D.C., and launched an effort to have every Member build a house in his or her congressional district.

I'd just come home after a bad round of golf.

"I'll never hit my 3-wood straight again the rest of my life!"

Gretchen Stelten

My mother listened and offered support. But she never left any room for self pity.

"The greens were so hard it was like trying to stop an approach shot on concrete."

Don't look for something or someone to blame. You'll do a lot better tomorrow.

"But I pushed every putt to the right of the cup."

That's just a little bump in the road. You're not a quitter. We'll just have to hit the practice green early tomorrow.

I got the message. It's not the problem that's important. It's what I do with it.

Where did my mother get all that wisdom?

Kathy Whitworth

Kathy Whitworth
SEVEN-TIME PLAYER OF THE YEAR
LADIES PROFESSIONAL GOLF ASSOCIATION

"Bob, little John David will walk with you to school." My mother's instruction about my first day in first grade was very clear—I would walk with Bob, my older brother, who was entering third grade.

We had just moved to Springfield, Missouri, where my father had a new job. Mom had a babe in arms (Wesley), a new home to organize, and two "big boys" who were heading off to the little school about a half mile's walk from the dusty, unpaved street that separated our front yard from a farm pasture. This was a time and place, of course, when safety from "strangers" wasn't an issue; children were safe walking to school.

But Bob's idea of opening day in third grade didn't include having little John David tag along. I got the message as we walked. Crestfallen, I decided to head back home.

"Now you've done it, Son," Mom said, her voice loving but firm. "Now you'll have to follow the road by yourself. Just keep walking until you come to the school."

Walk myself to school? Go inside and tell them I needed an education? Gulp! But I did it. After all, Mom was depending on me to be a big boy. Later in life, I realized that if I hadn't made it there on the second try, Mom would have

Betty Jane Trout

taken me there herself, with Baby Wesley in tow.

Lesson learned: at some point, each of us must take responsibility for ourselves.

John Ashcroft
UNITED STATES SENATOR

So many people think everything went right for me in 1996 because I won the National League Most Valuable Player Award. I did have a career year I never even dreamed of having, and we won the NL West title, so it was a great year.

But it wasn't perfect. In June, I was in one of the worst slumps of my career.

Every night when I was struggling, my mother would call me, no matter where I was, and I have to admit I didn't always want to hear from her. Sometimes she'd make me so mad I'd have to hang up on her. It was frustrating. She'd say, "I've seen your swing as much as anybody. I've seen it your whole life. So I know when it's right and when it's wrong."

I didn't like hearing her words, but it turned out she was right, as usual. She knew what was

Diane Borowski

wrong with me, and she helped me get through it in her own way. I mean, she's not exactly a hitting coach, but she did help me.

To be perfectly honest, I still wouldn't want her to call me every night, telling me how to do my job. But I know she will. She's my mother.

Ken Caminiti
San Diego Padres
National League Most Valuable Player 1996

I'm fourteen years old and my knee is busted. Again. I'm lying in a hospital bed. Just had my knee operated on. I open my eyes and who do I see? My mother! How refreshing to have her face there before my eyes. Somebody who loves me.

And she's not there just as my mother. That would be plenty. But she's also there as my nurse. She's taken a day off from her job, just to take care of her "Mama's Boy."

Yeah, I guess you could call me that. But it was always the whole family—Dad, Mom, my sisters. They all came to my games. All the college games. They were always there for me.

But it was my mother, the nurse, whom I saw first when I opened my eyes in the hospital. One shoulder operation. Four or five knee operations.

How good to see your face, Mama. Every time.

Charlie Ward
HEISMAN TROPHY WINNER
FLORIDA STATE UNIVERSITY

"Can you get that kid out of the way so we can continue this practice drill?" The voice had a hollow bitterness that reflected his anxiety to get this golf clinic over with. The cigar-sucking ex-marine was in over his head.

The ladies were lined up around the goalpost of the football field working on their weight shift during the downswing. It was not a pretty sight as steel shafts flashed and balls were launched in all angles.

"Stop, hold it!" he bellowed out of the side of his mouth as his cigar anchored the other side. "Would somebody tell this kid to get out of the way!" My mom, somewhat embarrassed, quietly strolled out to the forty-yard line and told me to go sit down in the bleachers and wait a few more minutes and we could go home. I took my seat and watched as thirteen women finished their golf lesson. What a stupid game this was.

I returned to that field many more times, not for football practice but to hit golf balls as my mom wearily went through the motions of learning this game. I actually learned to like the solitude and the challenge of the sport. I was hooked.

Mom would take me to the course every day

during the summer. It was my baby-sitter and I couldn't wait to smell the fresh cut grass and make my tracks in the early dew. I would stay until dark waiting for the flashing headlights to signal her return. I would regale her with stories of wonderful 3-irons to small greens and forty-foot putts that just missed. Mom would listen and take me again the next day to my newfound sanctuary.

I had been playing a year and entered a tournament at Fairmont Park golf course where I once was a nuisance. It was a two-day tournament and the final round was played on Sunday, early in May. In my anxiety to do well in my first tournament I completely forgot that

113

Gretchen Stelten

this was Mother's Day, and I was without an offering for my mom.

As we drove to the course I told her how much I appreciated her spending most of her waking hours driving me back and forth to the golf course and I said that to show my appreciation I would win this tournament for her on Mother's Day. The alternative of losing the tournament and ending up with no gift never entered my prepubescent mind.

The day was long and full of bad management on my part, but somehow I kept making putts and I continued to stumble forward. We arrived at the last hole and a well-worn volunteer marshal with a red windbreaker informed me that I needed par on the last hole to win the tournament! The pressure seized my throat and shortened my stride.

I remember having a putt about three feet long, slightly downhill and to the left, for my par. I looked up, and there in the gallery was my mother, smiling as if she knew this was her gift. I pretended I didn't see her and went about my business like the pros did on television.

As I got over the putt, it got very quiet inside my head. The only thing I could hear was my racing heartbeat. I stroked the putt with conviction and sympathy for the line. That three-foot putt took an eternity to get there and a lifetime to forget. It missed on the left.

I congratulated my playing partner who had won, and turned to find my mom standing there with her hands cupped over her mouth. That was the first time I remember failing at anything. Golf has a way of keeping one humble.

I didn't know what to do, but Mom reached out and put her arms around me. "I'm sorry I didn't win this for you on Mother's Day. I feel awful right now," I blurted out.

"You gave it all you have and just about won the first tournament you entered," she said. "You will, in time, realize the importance of failure."

My mother, once again, had turned a bump in the road of growing up into a wonderful lesson about life.

Gary McCord
CBS GOLF ANALYST AND AUTHOR

Motherhood is *not* for the fainthearted.
Used frogs, skinned knees, and the
insults of teenage girls are not meant for
the wimpy.

Danielle Steele

There never was a child so lovely but his
mother was glad to get him asleep.
Ralph Waldo Emerson

My mother had a great deal of trouble
with me, but I think she enjoyed it.
Mark Twain

A daughter is a woman that cares about
where she came from and takes care of
them that took care of her.
Toni Morrison

A Family Album

*M*y mother, the perennial worrier. After my father died, I would come home on leave to visit Mom and she would say, "Colin, take the book to the bank so they can show my interest."

And I would explain, "Mom, you don't have to do that. The bank will post the interest on the statement they mail you. The interest isn't going anywhere."

"How do you know they won't 'tief me?" she would say, using an old Jamaican expression for stealing. She would go to the bedroom, fish out an old lace-covered pink candy box from under the bed, and hand me the bank book.

I would dutifully trot down to the bank, stand in line, and say, "Will you please post the interest on this account?"

"Of course, Colonel Powell. But we show it on the statement. That can save you a trip down here."

"No," I would say, "my mother has to see those red numbers you print sideways to show the interest." And, I wanted to add, to prove you didn't 'tief her.

Colin Powell
FORMER CHAIRMAN, JOINT CHIEFS OF STAFF

Linda Mitchell

*F*ollowing my father's death, my mother got a job as a seamstress to support my sister, Elaine, and me. She became both mother and father. My mother's strength during my childhood and throughout my life has served as a powerful lesson to me.

Hard work pays off; love involves dedication and selflessness. These and many other virtues are essential to good family life.

One of my favorite memories from childhood is the hours I spent leafing through the photo album my mother brought with her from Italy. She used to sit down with me and tell the stories of the people and places on each page. Later on I would flip through the album by myself and study all of the details in each photo. When I finally made my first trip to Tonadico with my mother and sister in 1957, I was twenty-nine years old. What surprised me was that I instantaneously felt right at home. Because of the photos I felt as if I had been there before! I have been back to Tonadico many times, and each time I feel at home.

For my mother, teaching Elaine and me about the importance of family was essential.

I have always felt blessed to have come from a loving family, and my heart goes out to those who do not share the same experience. I believe, however, as my mother always has, that family goes well beyond blood lines.

Family is the human community, the Christian community, and we must learn to love one another as a family. Like any family, we have our disagreements, but in the end we are bonded together.

Joseph Cardinal Bernardin

Joseph Cardinal Bernardin
FORMER ARCHBISHOP OF CHICAGO

121

Abe Gurvin

*L*et me begin by confessing that I loathe mall shopping.

So as my Cuban mother eased her Tupperware-blue 1974 Buick into a parking lot of holiday shoppers, I felt near-despair at the scene before us: a teeming sea of vehicles trapped in parking lot purgatory.

"Mami, maybe we should head home. We'll never get a parking space on a holiday weekend."

I offered my most guileless smile.

With a suspicious sideways glance, she gripped the steering wheel a little tighter, adjusted the phone book beneath her hips, and quipped, "Sure we will. I'm an immigrant—we *make* a space. Besides, I've got parking radar."

Belying this confident avowal was the fact that we had just joined a serpentine line of cars winding through the overflowing lot.

"Great," I groused, "what's plan B?"

"Pray to our Lady of Perpetual Availability?" she proposed dryly.

Before I could respond, my septuagenarian mother started maneuvering her sedan around cars, to the predictable cacophony of car horns.

"Mami, what are you doing? You can't just break in line." I felt my voice rise an octave.

She rolled her eyes, hit the brakes, and pointed past me out the passenger window.

"I am trying to get *there*," she said with such urgency that I had to look.

It took me a moment to spot the red truck in the distance that was backing slowly out of a space and into the line of pressing cars.

"Mom, that truck is three aisles away from us!"

Oblivious to the honking of the bottlenecked vehicles behind us, she explained her strategy with a simple economy of words.

"I know that, honey. Now get out of the car and go stand in the parking space until I get there."

I didn't trust myself to speak. So she did.

"Well, God knows I wouldn't ask you to do anything I wouldn't do!"

I watched helplessly as my little Cuban mother put the car in park, released her seatbelt, and stepped out into the traffic, leaving both the door and my mouth wide open. Within moments, she reached and claimed the parking space made available by the departing red truck. I climbed over shopping bags into the driver's seat, then proceeded to inch along for an eternity, cursing my matriarchal DNA. If all the *Redbook* articles I'd

Truly mystifying

Mitzi Cartee

read were true, one day I would *be* this woman.

As I drew closer I could hear her, like a carnival barker.

"Back off mister—it's reserved! My daughter, she's coming! In the Buick!" Then I heard her calling me, fortissimo. "Sit up, honey, so they can see you!"

I groaned and sank deeper into the driver's seat. My mother stood her ground like a champ—her arms extended, one hand clutching her favorite faux patent leather handbag. I'll admit I was struck by a sense of bewildered awe at watching her ward off tons of steel with the sheer force of her personality and a Kmart purse. And I wasn't the only one spellbound: some cars had slowed to a crawl, drawn by the phenomenon of my mother.

I got out of the car and approached her, my jugular pounding much needed blood to my aching head.

"Mami, have you no shame?" I didn't know whether to throw my arms around her or kill her. (A reaction she would admit to having had toward me a time or two during my adolescence.)

"None." She patted my cheek. "And when you're my age, you won't, either."

Further discussion was postponed by an intrepid young stranger.

"Pardon me." A soft voice compelled me to look up and stare into an amused pair of hazel eyes.

"Is she your mama?" The woman before me was accompanied by a younger, male version of herself.

"Yes," I answered guardedly as I turned to face her. I had been watching my mother reach into the car for a bag.

"Lord, she's CRAZY," she said, with the sound of fascination, and humor, in her voice.

I looked over my shoulder to see if Mami was listening, "Look Miss—" I started protectively.

"What my sister meant was," the lanky young man pressed on for her, "*she reminds us of our mother.*" His sister nodded her head in agreement.

This was so unexpected. So human. It disarmed me completely and I was in this weakened condition when his sister whispered the coup de grace—"*God, I miss her.*"

I watched the two strangers for a moment as they walked away, their heads tilted together in intimacy, lost in their own reverie.

"You know, she's right," piped a familiar voice behind me.

I grinned despite myself.

"For the next fifteen years or so I'm going to drive you crazy—but after that, honey, *you're gonna miss me.*"

Carmen Agra Deedy
AUTHOR AND STORYTELLER

My mother likes to tell of her exasperation when caring for me as a baby. It seems that I did two things very well that tested my mother's famous patience. First, I drooled. According to my mother, I produced not just some occasional slime, but the Missouri River, more than my three brothers combined. I required several changes of clothing a day. Even worse, my nonstop slobber frequently compelled my mother to change her clothes as well. Nothing could stem the tide.

Second, Mom tells me that I had a tendency to bash my head against the crib at all hours of the night. I'd come up on all fours and, like a battering ram, repeatedly slam my noggin against the wooden crib slats. This, of course, was just as irritating as screaming. In a valiant effort to save my skull (and get some sleep),

Mom tried tying padding to the crib. No good. I'd tear it down. Would a padded hat slow down my fervor? Nope. I'd yank it off. The only solution seemed to be to allow me to bash until I fell asleep. Mom tells me that she would find me in the morning face down, head against the slats. Exhausted, I suppose, from my escape attempts. Mom thinks the head bashing explains a lot of things about me. I think my mother's patient care explains a lot more.

Gary Redenbacher
SPOKESPERSON
ORVILLE REDENBACHER'S GOURMET POPPING CORN

129

Carole Boyce

*M*y mother was born Virginia Marshall but was always called "Gig," a nickname which suited her lively, creative personality. In her youth, she came to the mountains of Virginia from her home on the Eastern Shore in order to teach school and ended up spending the rest of her life there, forever trying to civilize my father and his whole clan of whiskey-drinking Democrats. Yet she'd chosen Daddy over a well-bred gentleman from Richmond, a man who "went to the University of Virginia and never got over it," as she put it. In a few chosen words my mother could nail anybody. She led an uneventful life by most standards—after teaching she "just kept house," in her own words—yet she was powerfully interested in the news of the town and of the day and the lives of the stars as reported in the tabloids we eagerly grabbed each time we went up to the Piggly Wiggly. Everything she read or heard turned into an anecdote; each little trip into the world beyond our house yielded its little story. After I left home, I lived for her frequent, vivid telephone recitals. When she died, I realized I had lost not only my beloved mother, but my entire hometown as well.

Lee Smith

Lee Smith
NOVELIST

Mitzi Cartee

*W*hen I was a little girl, I asked my mother what she would like for Mother's Day.

"I don't need anything, Bonnie, just a little peace of mind."

Diane Borowski

Trying to be very clever, I took a piece of paper, and, in large letters, wrote the word "MIND" on it. Then I tore it in half, so it had rough edges where it had been torn. I placed half the paper in a small jewelry box, wrapped it in fancy paper, and tied it with a ribbon.

On Mother's Day, when my mother opened her present, she looked a little puzzled.

"That's what you said you wanted, Mom, a little piece of mind."

There may have been times when raising me was quite a challenge, but I was very lucky. My mother was always there for me, no matter what the circumstances. As I try to find the right mix, the right formula for being a good mother to my child, she is my role model.

Bonnie Blair

OLYMPIC GOLD MEDALIST, SPEED SKATING

*A*s we all know, it is our mothers who provide the nurture and guidance that we all need to get through the early stages of life, and a lot of this nurturing and guidance takes place in the kitchen.

One of my fondest memories relates to one of those kitchen times when I was age six. My mother was making a cake and had just poured the batter into the pan. I was industriously using my finger to wipe the extra batter off the sides of the bowl, which unfortunately did not please her.

In a kindly but firm tone she said,

Diane Borowski

"Jack, use your head." Not sensing the true intent of her words, I did exactly that and proceeded to put my face into the bowl and lick the sides. As only a mother could, she accepted this strange turn of events with the grace that she always showed, in the kitchen and out.

John Wieland

John Wieland
OWNER, JOHN WIELAND HOMES

133

Leavenworth Jackson

$\mathcal{M}$y mother was a striking beauty who left the world a more beautiful place than she found it. She grew lovely flowers, did the finest needlepoint I have ever seen, and knew how to keep an exquisite home.

I understand her better now than I did then. I certainly did not appreciate all the pressures she must have felt until I also became a mother. She taught me a great deal, although neither of us realized it at the time. Probably her most important lesson was an inadvertent one. You have two choices in life: You can like what you do, or you can dislike it. I have chosen to like it.

Barbara Bush

135

Barbara Bush
FORMER FIRST LADY AND AUTHOR

*D*id you ever wake up early on Mother's Day and suddenly realize you didn't have a present for your mother? Yikes! Panic time!

Before the alarm went off, before anyone was awake, I slipped on a jacket and quietly tiptoed out the door. *I can just gather some of these purple lilacs before anyone wakes up,* I thought, carefully breaking off a few blooms.

Uh-oh! I see somebody moving in the kitchen. I'll just stuff these lilacs into my jacket pocket so they can't be seen. And I'll walk in the door like nothing is going on.

Inside the house I found an empty bottle. I quickly removed the flowers from my jacket pocket and popped them into the bottle, just in time, as my mother entered the room.

"Happy Mother's Day," I cried, proudly holding out the bottle of green sticks, with just a few purple petals clinging stubbornly to the stems. Most of the flower petals were still in my pocket!

We all had a good laugh, and my mother thanked me and gave me a big hug.

How do mothers know just the right thing to do?

Amy Chow
OLYMPIC GOLD & SILVER MEDALIST, GYMNASTICS

Homer L. Springer, Jr.

Homer L. Springer, Jr.

One of my mother's favorite stories:

My brother and I shared a bedroom when we were very small. I was still in a crib. My brother, Don, was fourteen months older and had his own "big boy's" bed.

In the middle of the night, Don would climb out of bed and roam the house, finding some toys to play with. I guess I would hear him sometimes and wish I could go with him. Eventually, my mother would run him down and return him to his bed.

One night, as my exasperated mother returned her wandering son to his room one more time, she gazed at me, apparently sound asleep. But I must have been listening.

She said to Don, "Why can't you be good like your brother Kent is, and stay in bed all night?"

My mother was shocked when I opened my eyes and exclaimed loudly, "I...tan't...dit...out!"

Kent "Oz" Nelson
RETIRED CHAIRMAN AND CEO
UNITED PARCEL SERVICE

$\mathcal{M}$uch to my mother's dismay, the game with which I first became enamored was football. Bud Wilkinson, later famous as both player and coach, lived on my Minneapolis block, and as kids we played all games. Football was the neighborhood favorite, and Bud was our captain, coach, and right guard. I was the quarterback because he said I was the only one who could remember the signals. We had only one signal, really—22—which called for everyone to run for daylight. In the ensuing scrimmage, bruises were received, knees skinned, eyes blackened, even teeth lost. My mother, a woman of tremendous spirit and herself a formidable competitor, admired my spunk in playing football with my male peers, but she deplored the conditions in which I often came home.

Bud finally told me there was no future for me in football because I was too short and too slow; besides, I was always banging my legs and tearing my clothes.

I remember coming home and telling my mother of his harsh verdict, and to this day I can see her looking heavenward and saying, "Amen, amen."

Patty Berg
<small>Ladies Professional Golf Association Hall of Fame</small>

FROM A HABITAT HOMEOWNER

Some kids bring home stray animals. We always brought home kids.

But my mother didn't mind. The welcome mat was always out at our house. All the neighbors referred to our house as "The Ranch."

Every Sunday, after church, all the kids came to our house. Sometimes there would be as many as twenty children in our home at one time—laughing, singing, playing games. My brothers played bass guitar, drums, and piano, and composed songs. So we had a continuous talent show, starring all our friends!

Somehow my mother always had enough food to feed everyone. She was, and is, a loving, caring, giving person.

Those were happy times that I will always cherish. And I thank my mother for teaching me the importance of *family*.

My husband, Larry, and our four children have just moved into our first home—a Habitat home, built by hundreds of wonderful volunteers. I will do my very best to fill our home with the same love, and caring, and giving that my mother taught me as I was growing up.

Rita Miller

Rita Miller

Mitzi Cartee

INDEX OF ARTISTS AND ILLUSTRATORS

*O*ur special thanks to the following artists who generously donated their work.

CALL TO ACTION

HABITAT FOR HUMANITY INTERNATIONAL is a nonprofit, ecumenical Christian housing ministry that works in partnership with people everywhere to build simple, decent houses with families in need. Habitat's goal is to eliminate poverty housing and homelessness from the earth.

Habitat affiliates in all fifty states and more than sixty nations worldwide have built tens of thousands of houses that are sold to our partner families at no profit, with no interest charged on the mortgage. Partner family members invest hundreds of hours of their labor—sweat equity—building their houses and the houses of others. Habitat home ownership helps to break the cycle of poverty and brings new hope to families previously trapped in substandard, and often deplorable, living conditions.

You can be a part of this life-changing work! Join with the hundreds of thousands of Habitat volunteers around the world who have experienced the joy that comes from truly making a positive difference in the lives of families in need. Habitat welcomes your support through prayer, labor, and financial gifts. For more information, contact the Habitat for Humanity nearest you, or call 1-800-HABITAT, extension 551 or 552.

To make a tax deductible donation to Habitat work, please make your check payable to Habitat for Humanity International and mail it to:

Habitat for Humanity International
121 Habitat Street
Americus, Georgia 31709-3498

Diane Borowski

IN APPRECIATION

*T*o all the generous people who contributed a memento or a piece of artwork to this collection. You have *my* grateful thanks, and the thanks and gratitude of the *needy families* who will benefit from this book.

To all my friends who helped contact the authors and artists. I am deeply indebted to Coach Bobby Bowden (after contributing your own story), Helen Browder in Washington, Nancy Desmond, Kate Dodd, Bob Foley, Pete Foley, Anne Galvin in Cincinnati, Newt Gingrich (after contributing your own story), Laura Goodman, Christine Hausman, Mollie Hinckley, Patti and John Inman, Bob Jacobs, Bob Lowenberg, Larrie Del Martin, Phyllis Mueller, Mimi Nelson in Denver, Randy Raus, Dolores and Nick Riccardi, Nick Snider, Amy Sproull, Gretchen Stelten, Susan Taylor in San Diego, Phyllis Tickle, Betty Jane Trout, Gayle White, Ginny Williams, Carol Wintzinger, Dianne Wisner, Barry Witmer in Los Angeles, and Barbara Wooden.

To Kathy Landwehr at Peachtree Publishers, for your professional guidance and suggestions all along the way, for contacting authors and

146

artists, and for your contagious positive attitude. And to all the highly skilled professionals at Peachtree, for the unique expertise that each of you brought to the finished product.

And to my dearest Jeannie. You listened, guided, recommended, reviewed, supported. As with everything else in my life, this too was made better by your touch. Thank you, my love.

Gene Stelten
EDITOR

Gretchen Stelten

PERMISSIONS